Marcus Pfister

THE RAINBOW FISH

Translated by J. Alison James

Marcus Pfister

THE
RAINBOW FISH
and his Friends

North
South

CONTENTS

WOODSON

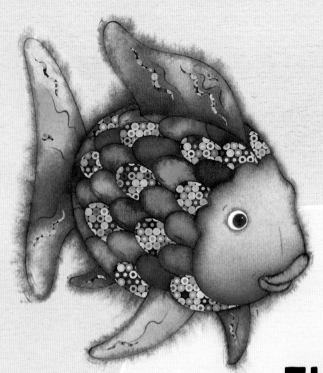

THE
RAINBOW FISH

A long way out in the deep blue sea there
lived a fish. Not just an ordinary fish, but
the most beautiful fish in the entire ocean.
His scales were every shade of blue and
green and purple, with sparkling silver scales
among them.

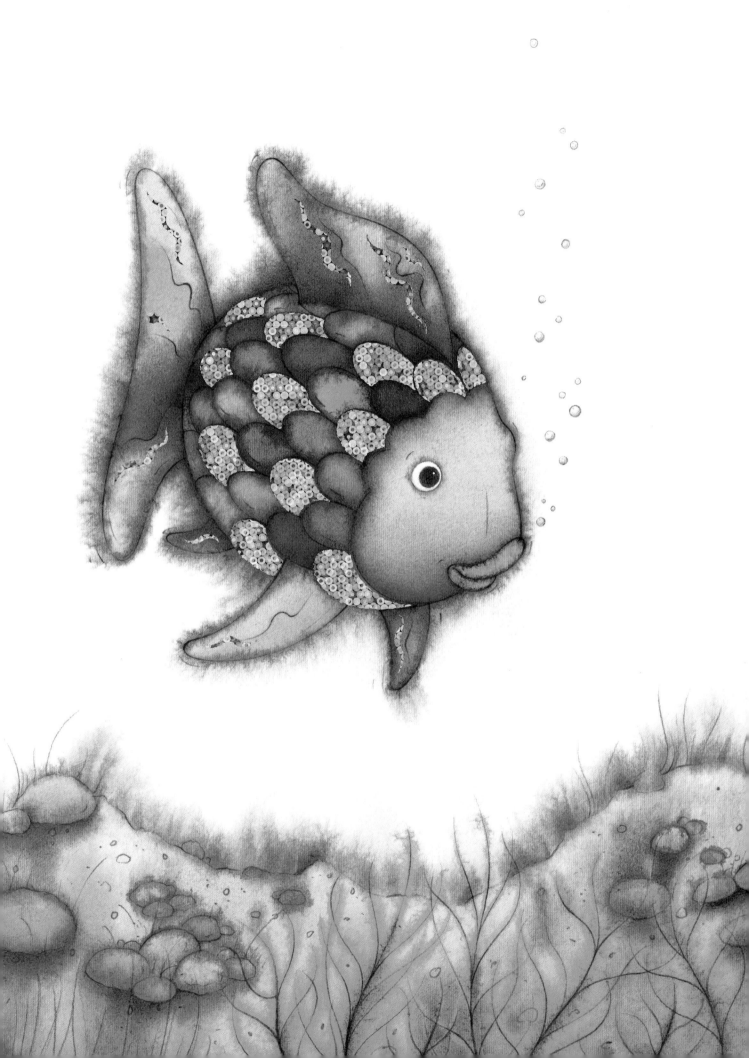

The other fish were amazed at his beauty. They called him Rainbow Fish. "Come on, Rainbow Fish," they would call. "Come and play with us!" But the Rainbow Fish would just glide past, proud and silent, letting his scales shimmer.

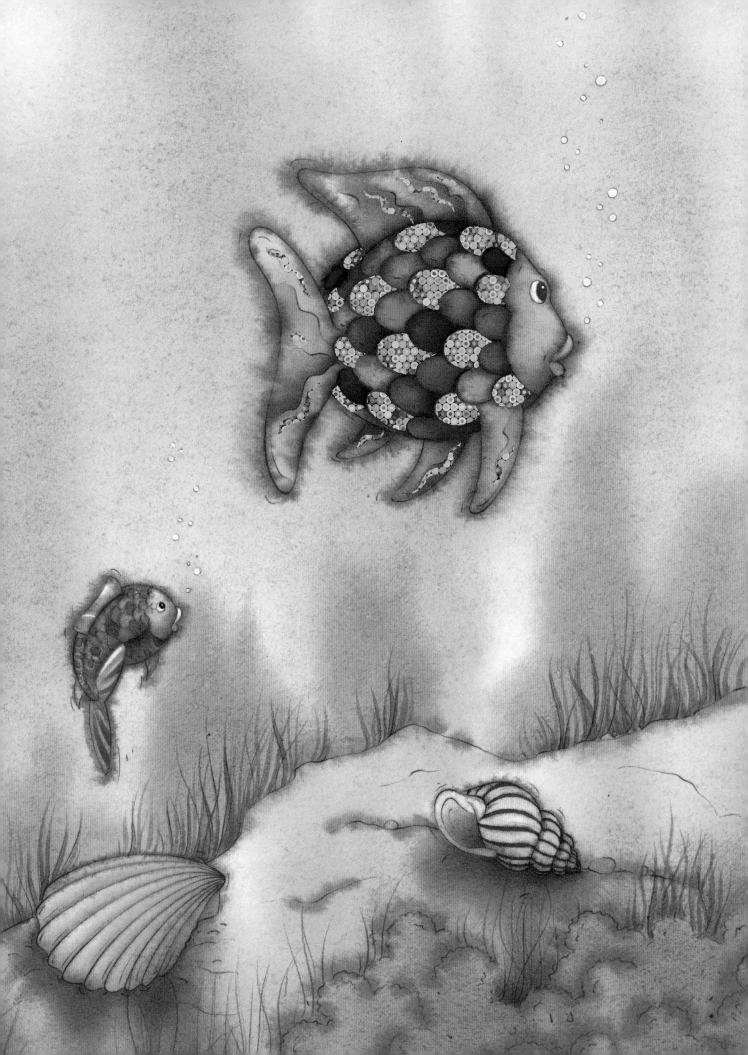

One day, a little blue fish followed after him.
"Rainbow Fish," he called, "wait for me!
Please give me one of your shiny scales. They
are so wonderful, and you have so many."

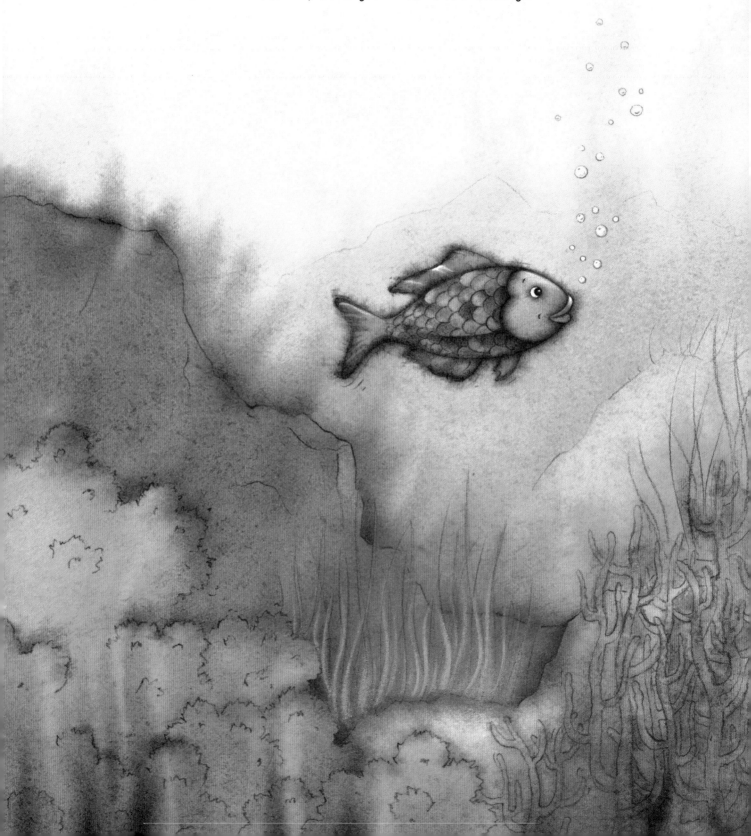

"You want me to give you one of my special scales? Who do you think you are?" cried the Rainbow Fish. "Get away from me!"

Shocked, the little blue fish swam away. He was so upset, he told all his friends what had happened. From then on, no one would have anything to do with the Rainbow Fish. They turned away when he swam by.

What good were the dazzling, shimmering scales with no one to admire them? Now he was the loneliest fish in the entire ocean.

One day he poured out his troubles to the starfish. "I really am beautiful. Why doesn't anybody like me?"

"I can't answer *that* for you," said the starfish. "But if you go beyond the coral reef to a deep cave you will find the wise octopus. Maybe she can help you."

The Rainbow Fish found the cave.
It was very dark inside and he couldn't
see anything. Then suddenly two eyes
caught him in their glare and the
octopus emerged from the darkness.

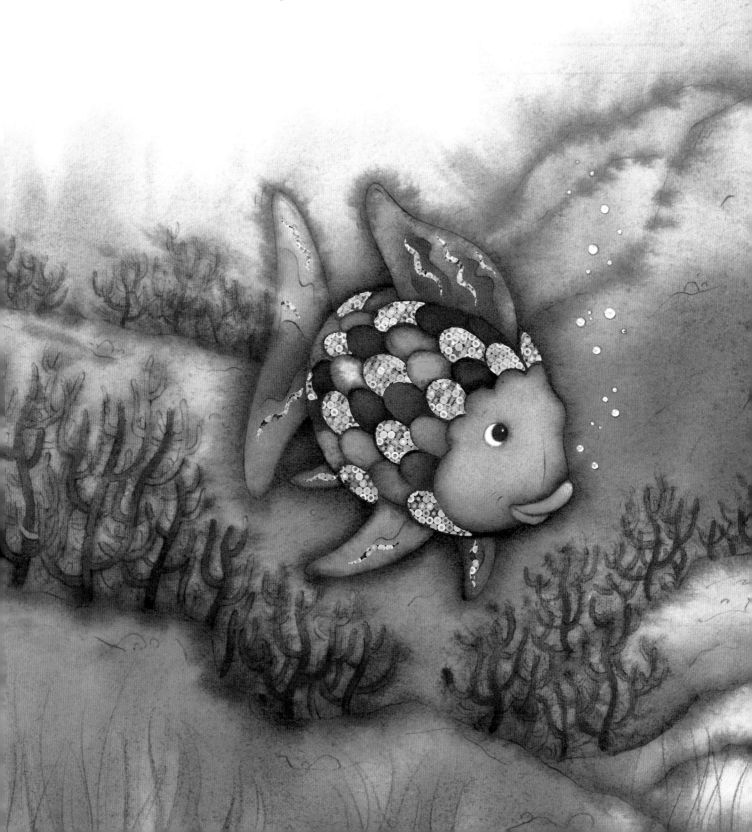

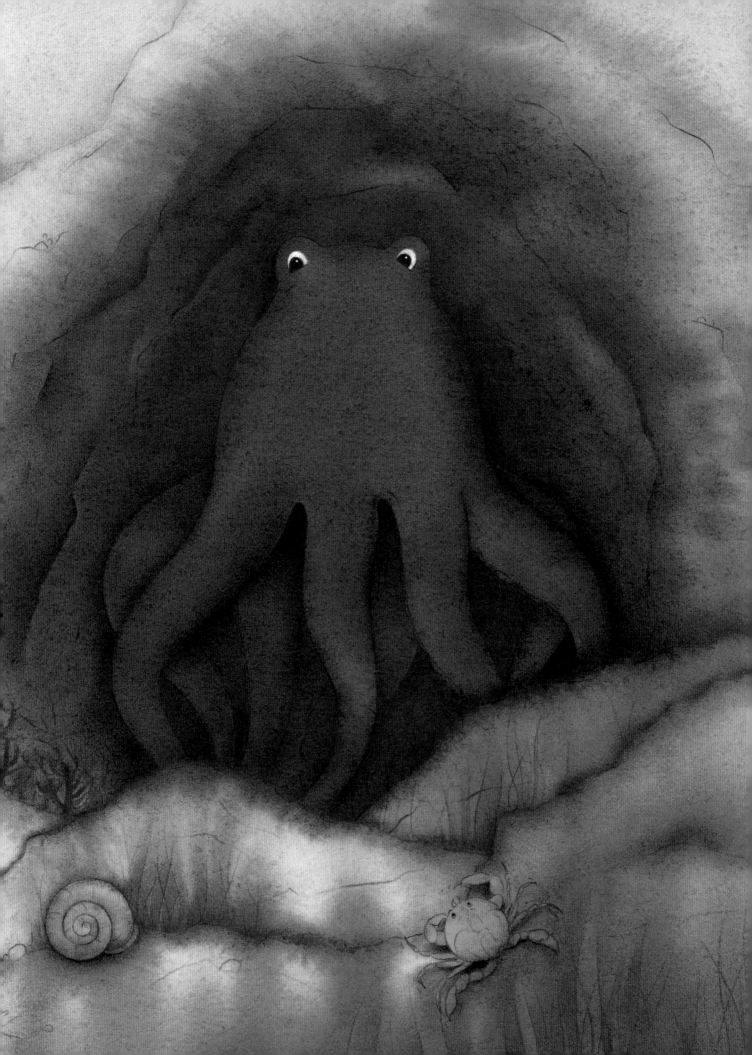

"I have been waiting for you," said the octopus with a deep voice. "The waves have told me your story. This is my advice. Give a glittering scale to each of the other fish. You will no longer be the most beautiful fish in the sea, but you will discover how to be happy."

"I can't . . ." the Rainbow Fish started to say, but the octopus had already disappeared into a dark cloud of ink.

Give away my scales? My beautiful shining scales? Never. How could I ever be happy without them?

Suddenly he felt the light touch of a fin.
The little blue fish was back!
"Rainbow Fish, please, don't be angry.
I just want one little scale."
The Rainbow Fish wavered. Only one
very very small shimmery scale, he thought.
Well, maybe I wouldn't miss just one.

Carefully the Rainbow Fish pulled out the smallest
scale and gave it to the little fish.

"Thank you! Thank you very much!" The little blue
fish bubbled playfully, as he tucked the shiny scale in
among his blue ones.

A rather peculiar feeling came over the Rainbow Fish.
For a long time he watched the little blue fish swim
back and forth with his new scale glittering in the water.

The little blue fish whizzed through the ocean with his scale flashing, so it didn't take long before the Rainbow Fish was surrounded by the other fish. Everyone wanted a glittering scale.

The Rainbow Fish shared his scales left and right. And the more he gave away, the more delighted he became. When the water around him filled with glimmering scales, he at last felt at home among the other fish.

Finally the Rainbow Fish had only one shining scale left. His most prized possessions had been given away, yet he was very happy.

"Come on, Rainbow Fish," they called. "Come and play with us!"

"Here I come," said the Rainbow Fish and, happy as a splash, he swam off to join his friends.

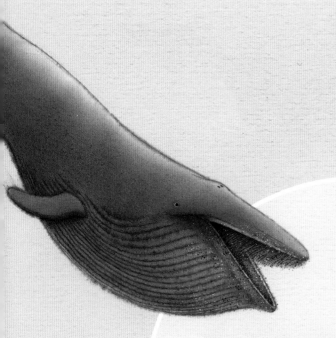

RAINBOW FISH
and the Big Blue Whale

A long way out in the deep blue sea,
Rainbow Fish and his friends swam happily
through the reef. Each of them had a glittering
silver scale-except for one little striped fish,
but he belonged to the group anyway.

When the fish were hungry, they ate tiny krill. There seemed to be endless supplies of the delicious shrimp. Rainbow Fish only needed to glide gently through the water with his mouth open to catch as many as he wanted. It was a wonderful life.

One day a gentle old whale swam by the reef and decided to stay. He liked the spot, since he too ate the krill that were so plentiful there. And he enjoyed being around the glittering fish. Often he drifted along, watching them for hours, admiring their beautiful silvery scales.

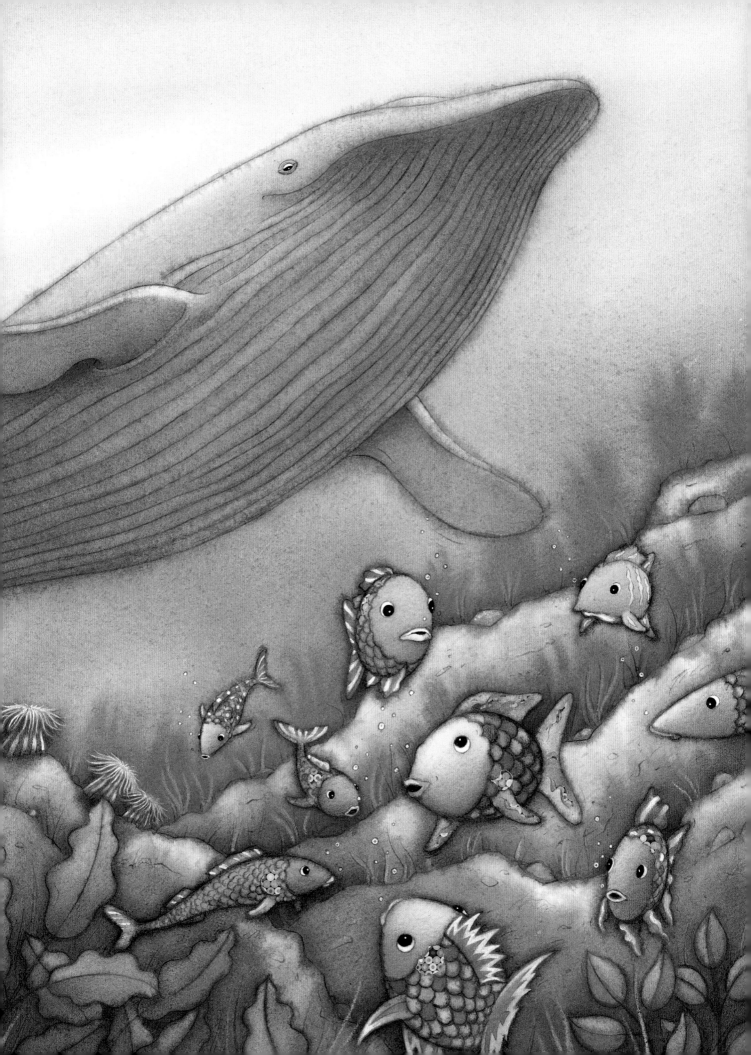

Before long, the fish with the jagged fins noticed the whale watching them.

"Why is he looking at us like that?" he asked the others. He was in a particularly bad mood that day. "See how he's staring at us?" he went on irritably. "Who knows what he's thinking?"

After that all the fish grew more and
more suspicious of the whale.

"Look at that giant mouth," said one.
"Soon the krill will all be gone."

Rainbow Fish began to worry. Until now
the fish had always been able to eat their
fill. What if the whale did eat up all the krill?
And why did he keep staring at them?
Was he planning to eat them, too?

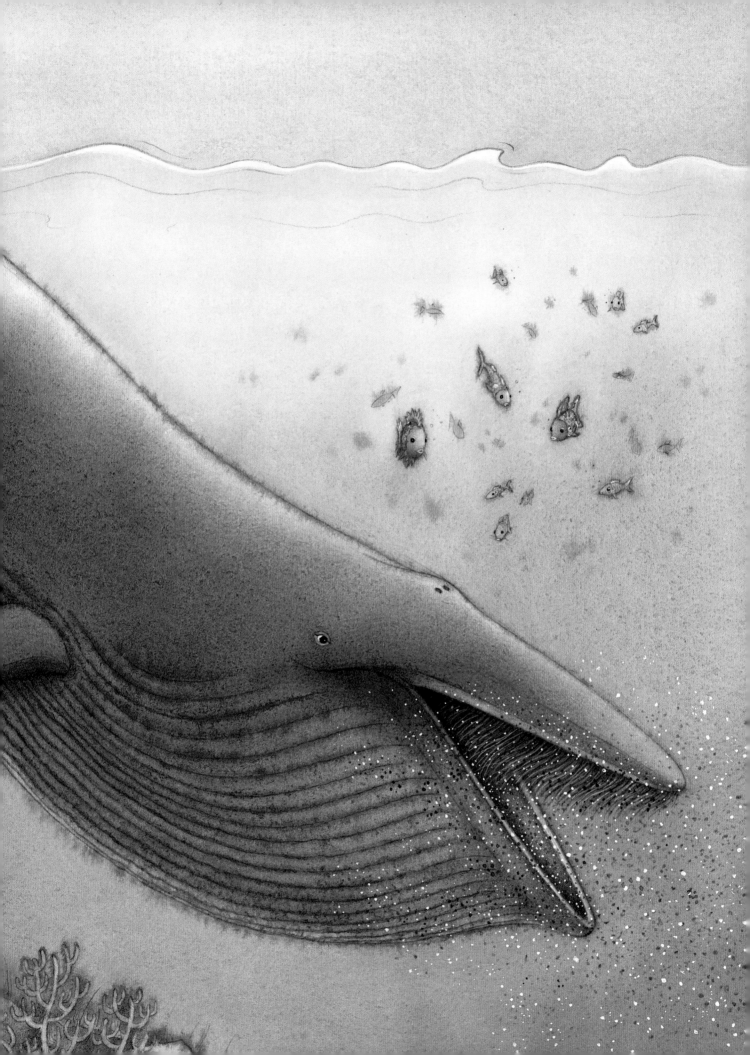

One day the whale swam quite near the school of glittering fish. Panicked, the fish with the jagged fins sounded the alarm.

"Look out!" he called. "The wicked whale is after us!"

When the whale heard that, he was hurt at first, but soon he grew very angry.

I'll show them! he thought. I'll teach them a lesson!

So the great blue whale shot into the middle of the school and lashed out with his gigantic tail, sweeping the sparkling fish in all directions.

The terrified fish fled, racing towards a crack in the reef for safety. But the whale didn't leave them alone. He followed Rainbow Fish and his friends all the way back to their cave.

The blue whale swam back and forth, casting sinister glances at the little fish.

They were trapped!

"I told you that whale was dangerous," whispered the fish with the jagged fins. "We have to watch out for him!"

After a while the whale calmed down. He made one last pass, then disappeared behind the reef.

Nervous, but driven by hunger, the fish cautiously left their cave and swam off in search of food. But the battle with the whale had left its mark: all the krill had been driven off.

"This is silly!" declared Rainbow Fish. "Before, we played happily in the sea. Now we hide in terror in our cave. Before, there was always enough food for everyone. Now we have nothing. We must make peace with the whale."

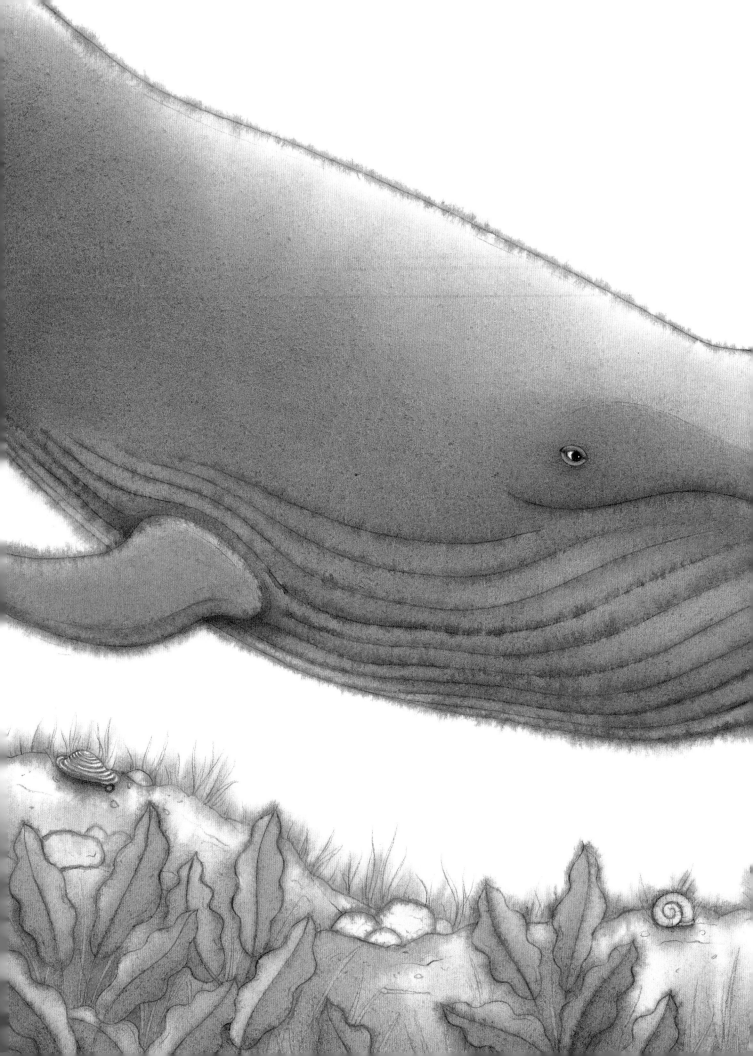

The other fish were all too afraid to approach the whale. It was up to Rainbow Fish.

The whale stared at Rainbow Fish suspiciously.

"Please, let's talk," said Rainbow Fish. "This fight was all a big mistake. It drove off the krill and now we're all hungry."

The two talked for a long time.

The whale told Rainbow Fish how hurt and angry their hostile words had made him. "I never meant to harm you," said the whale, "just scare you a little."

Rainbow Fish was ashamed. "I'm sorry," he said. "But when we saw you watching us all the time, we were afraid you might eat us."

The whale looked surprised. "I watched you only because your shining scales are so pretty," he said.

They both laughed.

"Come now," said the whale. "Let's find new hunting grounds."

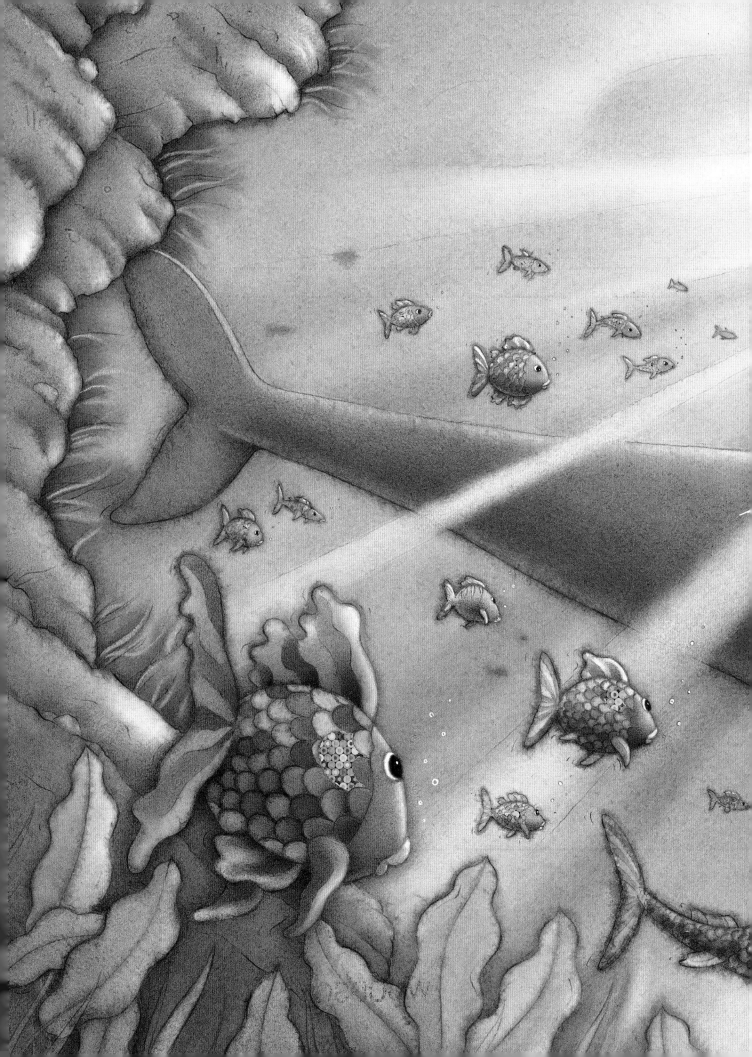

So Rainbow Fish and his friends, protected by their new friend the big blue whale, swam off together in search of a new home rich with krill. And before long, none of them could remember what the terrible fight had been about.

WOODSON

RAINBOW FISH
Discovers the
Deep Sea

A long way out in the deep blue sea, Rainbow Fish and his friends played happily near an underwater canyon. Over the edge, the seabed dropped deep down. No one knew how far.

"I would love to know what's down there," said Rainbow Fish to the little blue fish. "Who knows what's waiting to be discovered?"

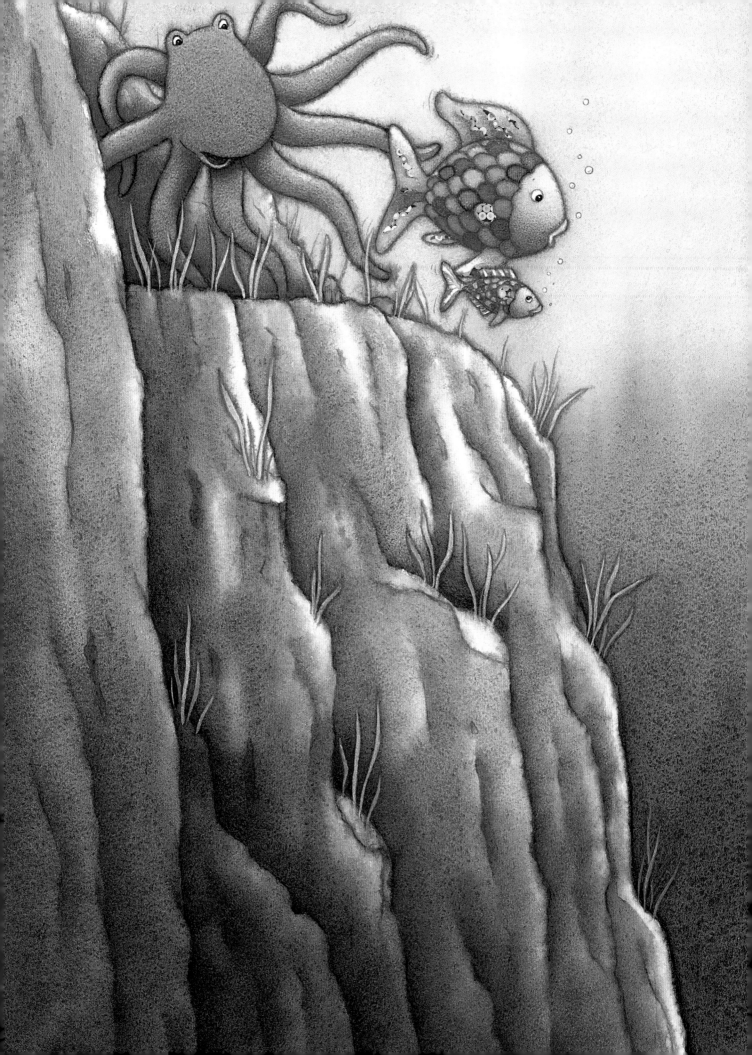

"If I were you, I'd stay up here," said the octopus. "I've heard that it's cold down there, and dark—and full of strange creatures nothing like us."

So Rainbow Fish had to be content to swim along the edge and stare down into the depths, wondering what was there.

One day a strong ocean current pulled Rainbow Fish's last sparkling silver scale right off. The scale drifted over the edge of the canyon wall and sank down and down and down into the darkness.

Rainbow Fish wanted to chase after it, but the little blue fish pulled him back. "No, Rainbow Fish!" he cried. "Please don't go after it. There are strange creatures down there."

"I'd like to meet them," said Rainbow Fish.

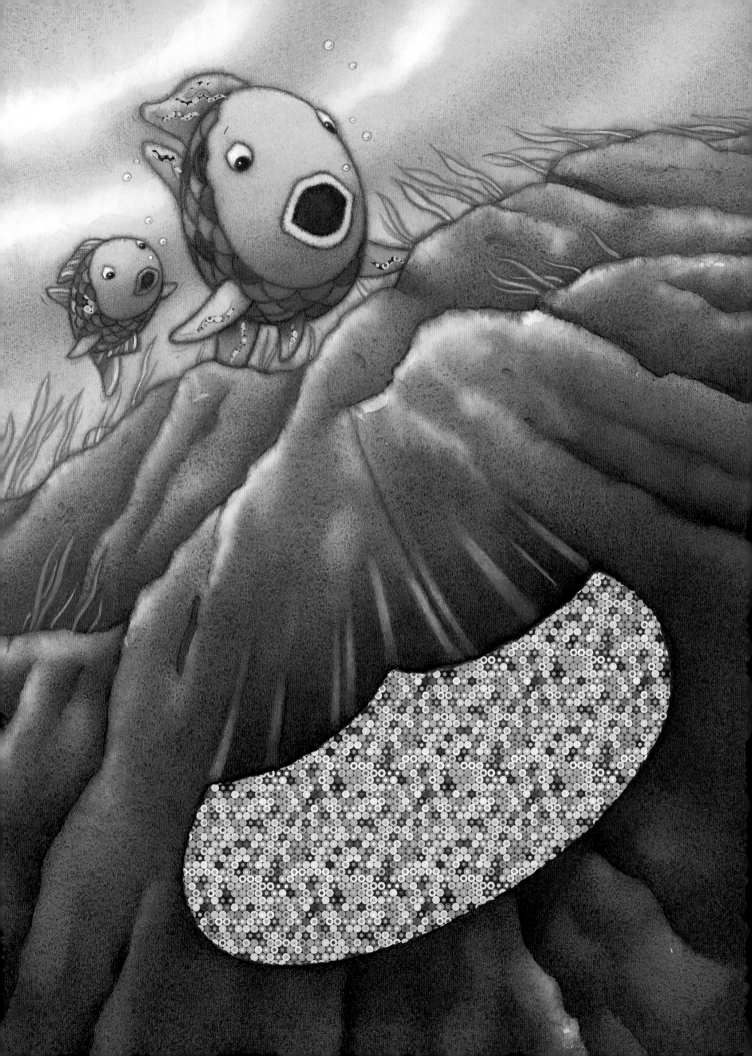

"Oh, dear," said the little blue fish. "Wait here. I'll get help."

But Rainbow Fish couldn't wait. As soon as his friend left, he dove down into the depths. He just had to find his scale.

Soon it was so dark that Rainbow Fish could see nothing except a tiny sparkling speck getting smaller and smaller and smaller below him. Rainbow Fish started to feel frightened.

Then suddenly it began to get light again. A glowing pink creature seemed to appear out of nowhere.

"Hello," said the creature. "I'm a firefly squid. Who are you? And what are you doing down here?"

Rainbow Fish swam closer. "I'm Rainbow Fish," he said. "I lost my sparkling silver scale, and I came down here to find it. You haven't seen it by any chance, have you?"

"I'm afraid not," said the squid. "But I can help you look."

So Rainbow Fish and the firefly squid set off to find the lost scale. Along the way, they met three glowing jellyfish.

"A sparkling silver scale?" said the jellyfish. "Yes! One drifted by this way. We played with it for a while. Then it drifted off again. We didn't know someone had lost it. If we had known that, we would have kept it for you."

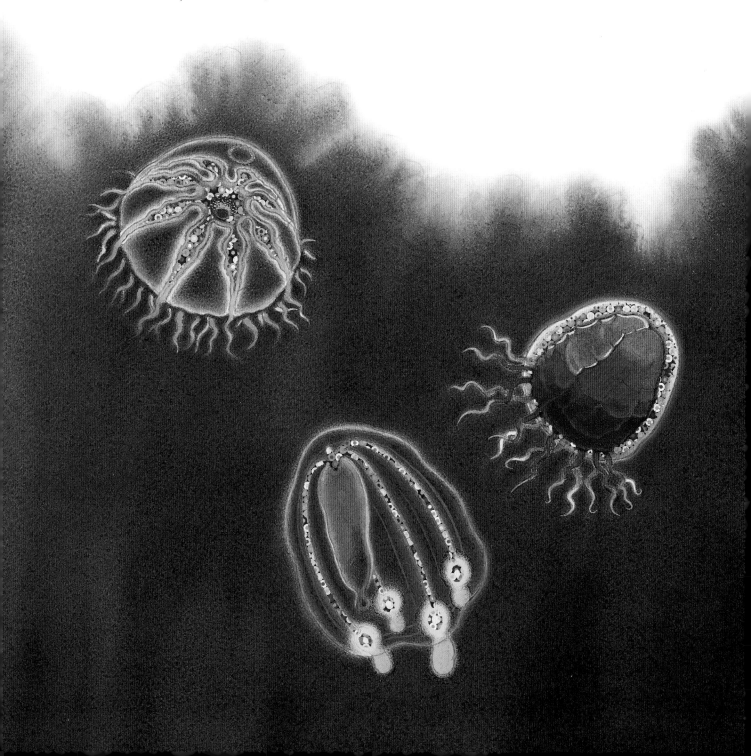

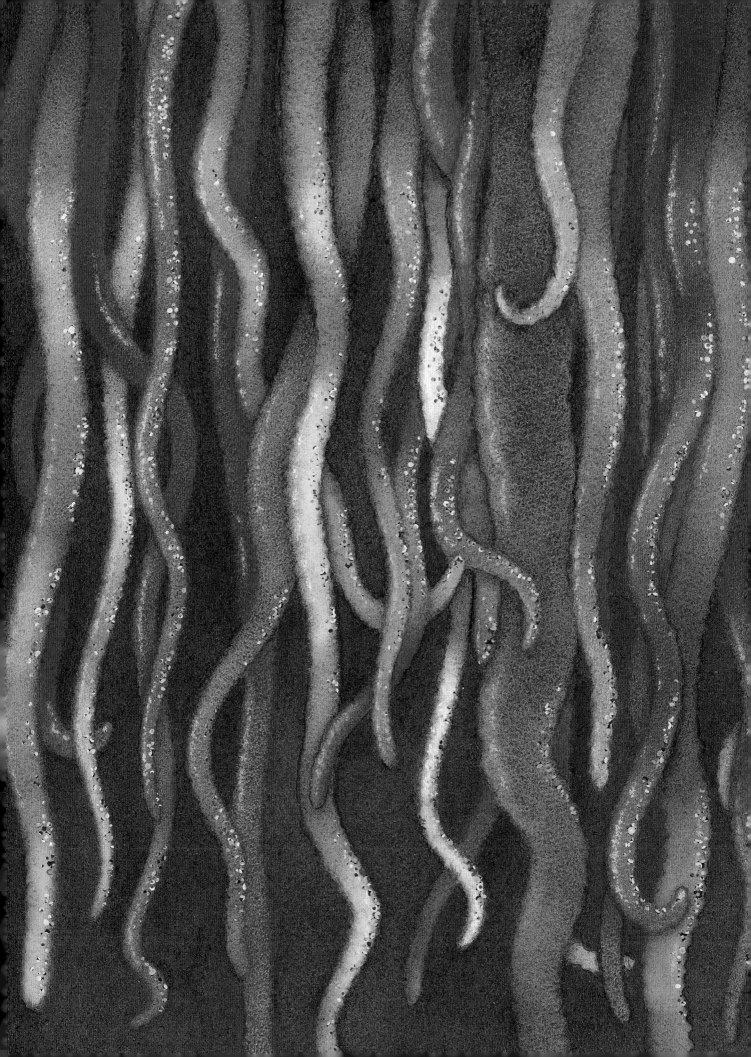

Rainbow Fish and the firefly squid swam deeper down. Suddenly, their way was blocked by a wavy curtain of bluish green tendrils.

"Watch out!" called the squid. "Those are the poisonous tendrils of a siphonophore!"

Rainbow Fish shivered. There was danger in the deep sea. "Have you seen my sparkling silver scale?" he asked shyly.

The siphonophore was rather rude. "Down here even the tiniest crabs glow and glisten," he mumbled. "How can I be expected to spot a single sparkling scale?"

"Don't feel bad," said the firefly squid. "He's just like that. Look—there's a sea slug. Maybe she's seen your scale."

But the sea slug hadn't seen anything. "Sorry," she said. "I wish I could help, but I don't see very well."

Rainbow Fish and the firefly squid swam down
farther, until they reached the seabed.
   "My scale must be around here somewhere,"
said Rainbow Fish. But it was very dark at
the bottom, and the squid's light was too weak
to show much.

"There's a dumbo octopus," said the firefly squid. "Come on. I'm sure she'll help us."

But the three of them still couldn't find the sparkling scale.

"I know what to do!" cried the dumbo octopus. "I'll just give you a new sparkling costume, Rainbow Fish." And she covered him in a shower of glitter so that Rainbow Fish glistened like never before.

"Thank you!" said Rainbow Fish. "It's beautiful! Truly! But I really want my own scale back again."

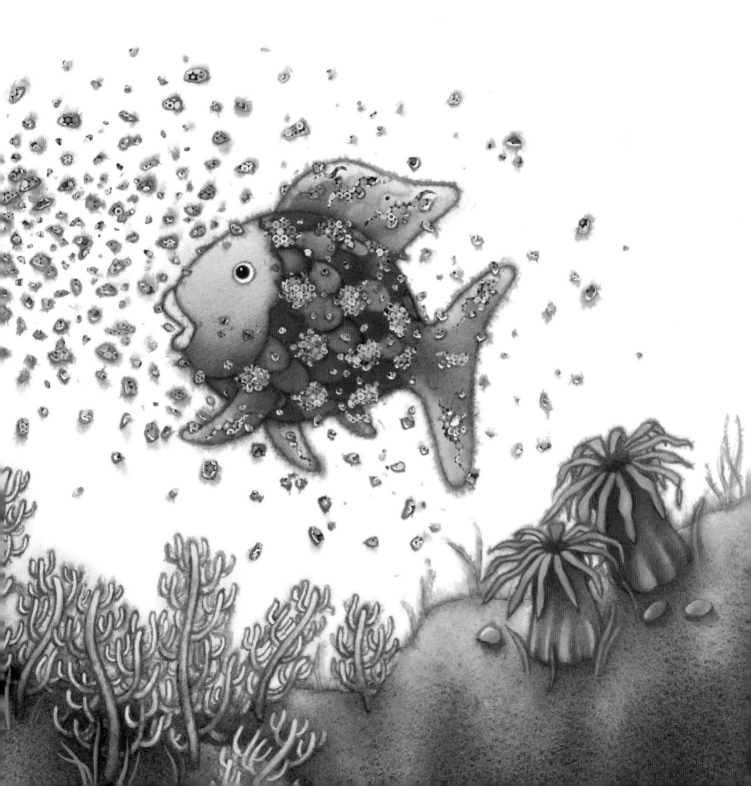

"Then we're going to need more light," said the firefly squid. He called to all the creatures of the deep sea—and they all came.

Together they lit up the seabed.

"Wow!" said Rainbow Fish. "It's beautiful down here."

Then everyone looked . . . and looked . . . and looked. They were just about to give up when the light from a lantern fish showed something glittering in the water.

"My scale!" cried Rainbow Fish, and everyone cheered.

"Oh, thank you!" Rainbow Fish told his new friends. "I would never have found it without you!"

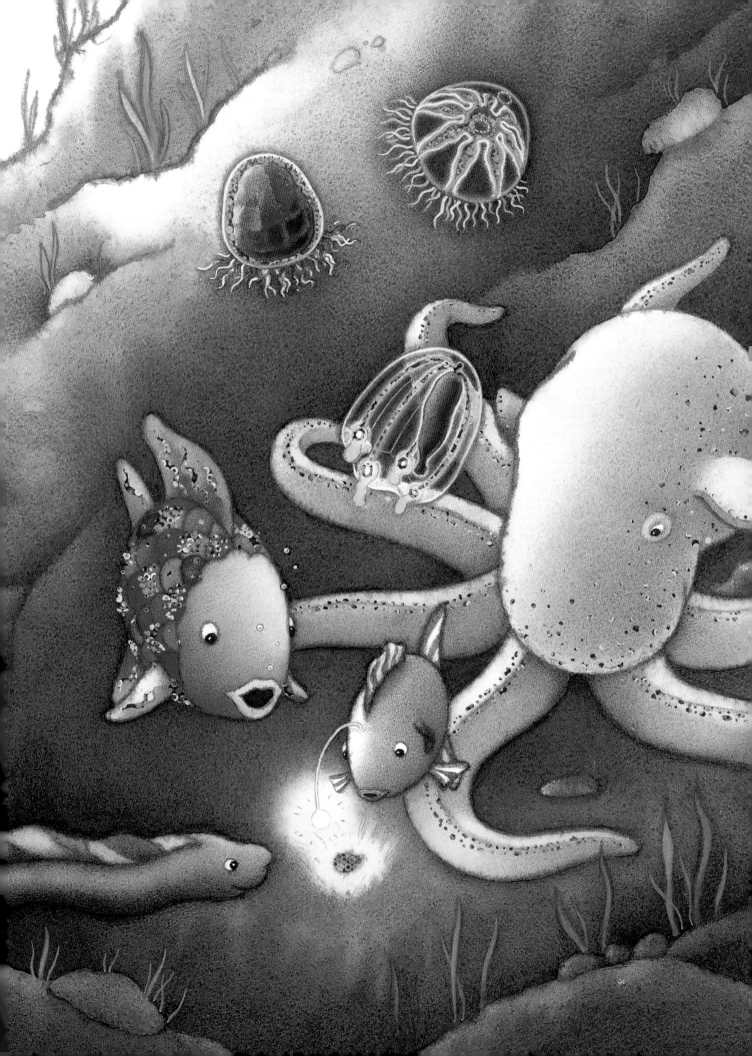

Rainbow Fish and the firefly squid swam up and up and up and up with the sparkling silver scale. Before they reached the top of the canyon, they had to part.

"Come visit us again," said the squid.

"I will," promised Rainbow Fish.

The little blue fish and all his other friends were waiting to welcome Rainbow Fish home. Everyone wanted to know what it was like down in the depths. "Was it scary?" they asked. "Were the creatures awful?"

"No!" said Rainbow Fish. "They were beautiful! They looked different, but they turned out to be wonderful friends. Just like you."

You Can't Win
Them All,
RAINBOW FISH

Rainbow Fish enjoyed drifting around in the sea.
    His home was the shining shoal, and he was happy
there among his friends.
    There had also been some additions to the shoal.
    Red Fin had joined them, and immediately she
and Rainbow Fish became good friends.
    "Come on, let's play hide-and-seek," said Red Fin.
"Will you be the first seeker, Rainbow Fish?"

Rainbow Fish agreed. He began to count up to
twenty while the other fish looked for hiding places.
   "I'm coming!" he shouted. "I'll find you in a fishy
flash! I hope you're well hidden."
   Rainbow Fish looked around. By now he knew most
of the hiding places, so he knew exactly what to
do and where to go.
   But this time he couldn't find anybody.

There, among the algae, wasn't that something moving?
Rainbow Fish swam closer without taking his eyes off
the area around him.

"I'm over here!" Red Fin shouted laughingly from behind.
"You swam right past me!"

"Where were you? I never even saw you," said Rainbow Fish
mystified.

"Not telling," said Red Fin. "Go and look for the others."

Rainbow Fish swam off toward the reef.

He searched and searched among the corals, and then at last . . .

"Hellooo! You didn't see me! I'm over here!" cried the fish with the jagged fins.

Rainbow Fish had missed finding him too.

The only one missing now was Little Blue.

Hmmm. Rainbow Fish had already searched all around the reef, behind the corals, and in the algae. The only place left was among the sea anemones.

"Just you wait, Little Blue, I'll find you. . . ."
"Where are you going? I'm hiding over here!" cried Little Blue.
"I don't believe this," Rainbow Fish thought. "I didn't find a single one! This has never happened to me before!"
But he kept his frustration to himself and said, "Your turn to be seeker, Little Blue."

Rainbow Fish was pleased with himself now.

Little Blue would never find him. Little Blue was still very young and didn't have much experience playing hide-and-seek.

"One, two, three . . . ," Little Blue began to count while the other fish hid themselves.

Rainbow Fish ducked down behind a bush of algae and didn't move a muscle.

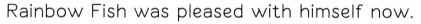

"Rainbow Fish, I can see you! You're hiding behind the algae!" cried Little Blue. "Come on out, Rainbow Fish. I've found you."

"I don't believe it!" said Rainbow Fish. "You can't possibly have seen me. You obviously didn't count up to twenty. It's not fair!"

All the other fish came out of their hiding places.

"Oh, come on, Rainbow Fish, it's only a game," said Red Fin, giving him a friendly poke in the ribs.

"What? Well, I think it's a dumb game, and I'm not playing!" said Rainbow Fish angrily, and he swam away.

"Can't we play anymore?" asked Little Blue sadly.
"I'm sorry, I was only trying to . . ."

"It's not your fault, Little Blue," said Red Fin.
"You didn't do anything wrong. I'll talk to him.
Don't worry. Everything is going to be all right."

Red Fin found Rainbow Fish near the reef.

"You were really unlucky this time, weren't you?" said Red Fin gently. "But you can't always win. It's only a game. And did you see the look in Little Blue's eyes? He was so proud that he'd found you. He's the one who always loses. And now you've spoiled all the fun for him. That's not fair."

Rainbow Fish listened in silence.

He knew Red Fin was right.

First, the other fish had simply found better hiding places than he had. Then he hadn't hidden himself well enough, and finally he'd been a poor sport.

"You're right." Rainbow Fish sighed. "I was acting like a poor sport. So now what do I do?"

"Come with me, apologize, and carry on with the game," said Red Fin warmly. "What else can you do?"

"I don't know if I'm brave enough to do that. It's all so embarrassing," said Rainbow Fish miserably.

"I know you pretty well," said Red Fin. "You know what you have to do. You'll make everything right again."

Together they went back to their friends. Rainbow Fish swam up to Little Blue.

"I'm sorry I was a poor sport, Little Blue. You're really good at hide-and-seek now. And I have to get used to it. . . . Will you give me another chance?"

"Yes!" said Little Blue with a big smile.

"My turn to count!" cried the fish with the jagged fins. "I'll find you in a fishy flash! I hope you're well hidden."

Good Night,
LITTLE
RAINBOW FISH

The Little Rainbow Fish couldn't sleep. His eyes simply wouldn't close. He tossed and turned in his watery bed of plants.

"I can't get to sleep," moaned Little Rainbow Fish.

"What's the trouble, darling?" asked Mommy.

"It's so dark."

"Don't be afraid!" said Mommy. "I'll send for the lantern fish. He'll shine his light for you until you fall asleep. Good night, Little Rainbow Fish."

"Could you stay with me for a while, Mommy?"
"I'll never leave your side, darling."
"Promise?"
"Cross my rainbow heart!"

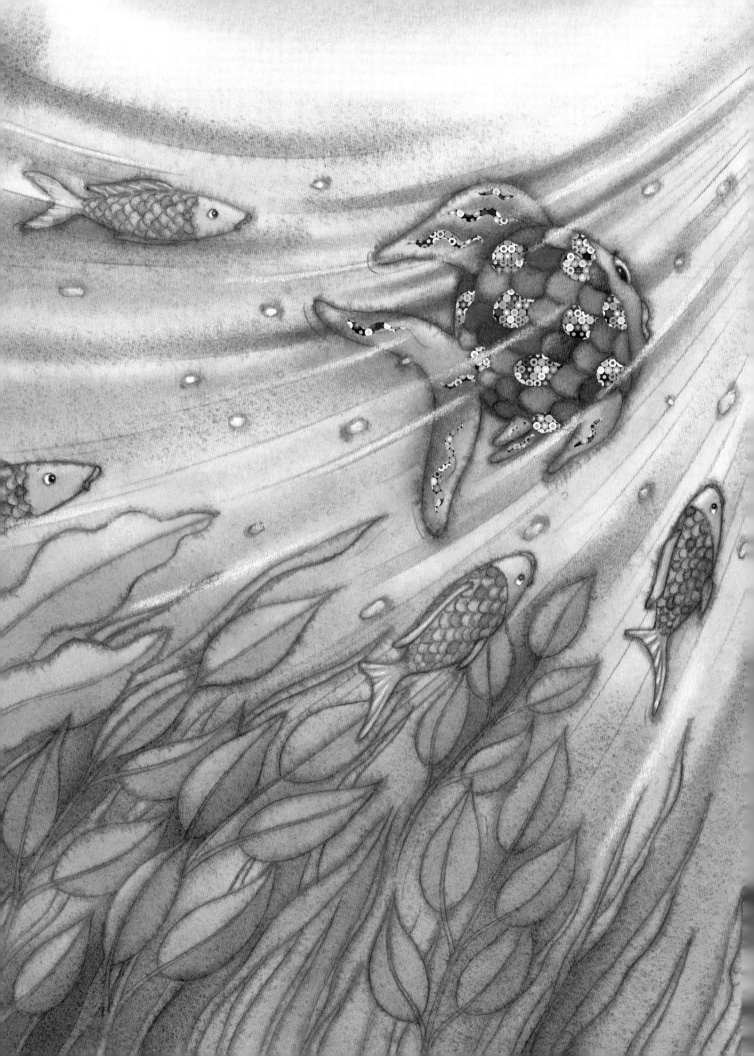

"But suppose the tide comes and takes me away?"

"Then I'll follow you faster than a swordfish can swim and bring you safely home again."

"And suppose I lose my way in
an octopus's cloud of ink?"

"Then I'll search for you, blow away
the black cloud, and take you home."

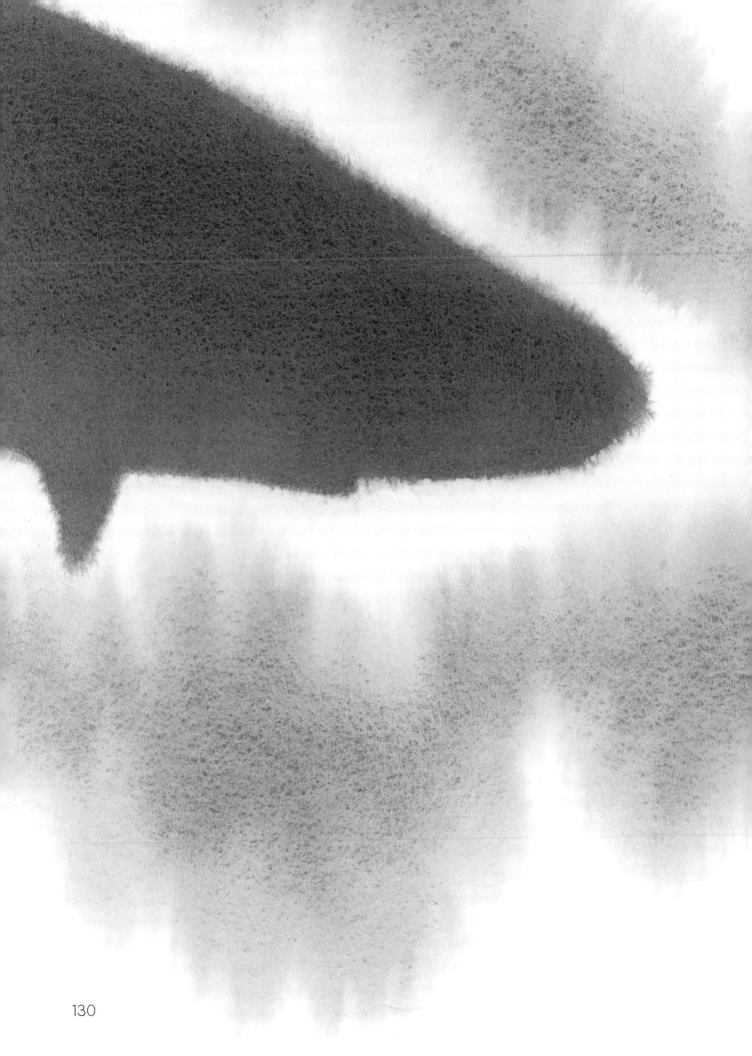

"And suppose a monster fish
comes to gobble me up?"

"Then the monster fish will have to face
me first! And I'll give him such a fright that
he'll swim away and never come back."

"And suppose I get caught in the arms of a poisonous jellyfish?"

"Then I'll nurse you until you're well
again, and the jellyfish will
get a nasty surprise."

"And suppose I have a bad dream tonight?"

"Then I'll take you in my fins and hold you very, very tight. Good night, darling."

"Good night, Mommy," murmured Little Rainbow Fish, and then he happily fell asleep.

FUN AND GAMES

RAINBOW FISH COOKIES

PREHEAT OVEN TO 350°F, REQUIRES ASSISTANCE FROM AN ADULT

★ Mix sugar and butter together in a bowl (using mixer). Beat until creamy

★ Add egg and lemon peel and stir till the mixture is smooth. Gradually add the flour and then knead the dough thoroughly. Place the dough in refrigerator for 15 minutes.

★ Sprinkle a thin layer of flour over your work surface.
Roll the dough out flat.
Cut out the cookies using fish-shaped cookie cutter.

★ Bake the cookies at 350°F on the center rack of your preheated oven. Bake for 15 minutes (until the cookies are golden-yellow). Let cool.

★ Decorate your cookies once cool. Mix the frosting together with food coloring. If necessary, add a little water. Finally, spread the glitter sprinkles over the icing and leave to dry.

INGREDIENTS

½ cup sugar

¾ cup butter

1 egg

1¾ cup flour

grated lemon peel (organic)

fish-shaped cookie cutter

frosting

blue food coloring

glitter sprinkles

COLOR IN THE RAINBOW FISH!

★ Parents, caregivers, teachers: You can use this image to make multiple copies.

CAN YOU FIND THE WAY?

★ The Rainbow Fish would like to visit his mother.
Can you show him the way?

FANTASTIC UNDERWATER WORLD

★ With a small sponge and bright water-colors, paint a sandy seabed on a piece of drawing paper.

★ Rinse well, then using the sponge again, paint light-blue water above it.

★ Let it all dry for about 20 minutes. Using your crayons, draw brightly colored plants and creatures of the undersea world.

★ Perhaps the Rainbow Fish is hiding somewhere in the picture. Or maybe there's a submarine or a mermaid gliding through the water.

Have fun creating a fascinating underwater world of your own!

MATERIALS

drawing pad

watercolor paints

small sponge

crayons

RAINBOW FISH BOOKMARK

REQUIRES ASSISTANCE FROM AN ADULT

★ Draw a fish on a sheet of white paper. Ask an adult to cut out your fish drawing. Place the fish shape on the blue felt and ask an adult to use your fish drawing as a stencil to cut the blue felt into the same fish shape. Cut the fabric remnants into "scales" for the fish and use the yellow fabric to cut out the "mouth" of the fish.

★ Ask an adult to cut two equal, right-angle triangles out of the cardboard, making sure that the two right angles are the same size.

★ Finally, ask an adult to sew or staple together the two sides that form the right angles so they can fit onto the corner of a page in a book.

★ Glue the blue felt fish onto the two joined-together triangles, then glue the scales onto the fish and decorate the fish with sequins. Glue on the googly eye and the yellow mouth.

When the fish are nicely dried, you can use it as a bookmark.

MATERIALS

pencil

white paper

scissors

cardboard

blue felt

fabric remnants (blue, green, red, purple, yellow)

sewing machine or stapler

glue

sequins

googly eye

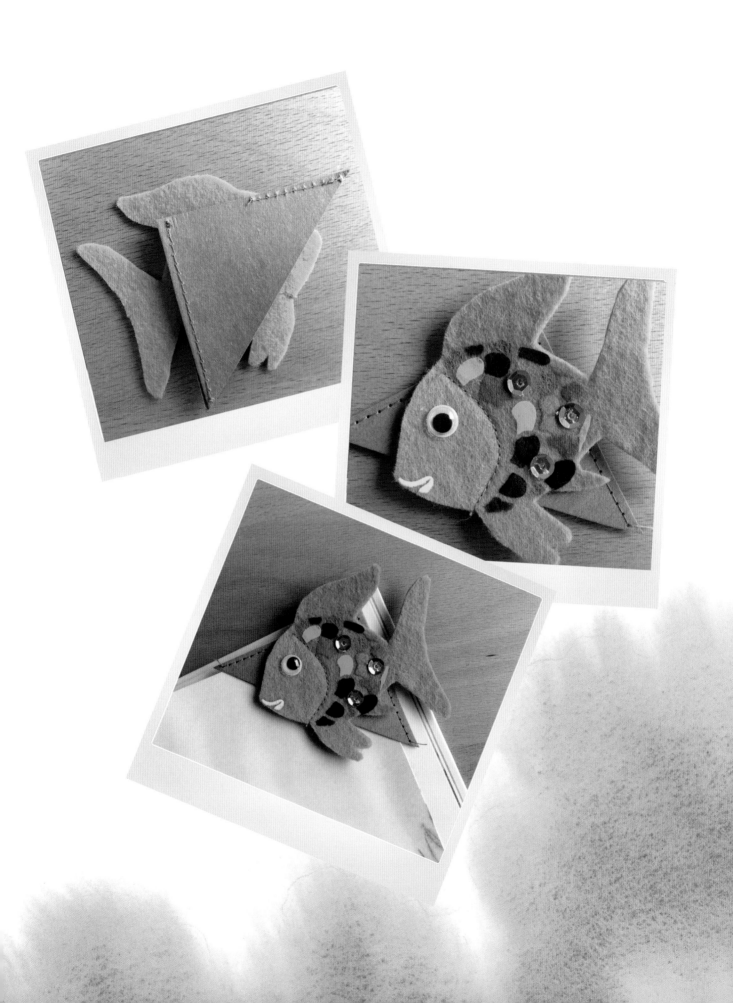

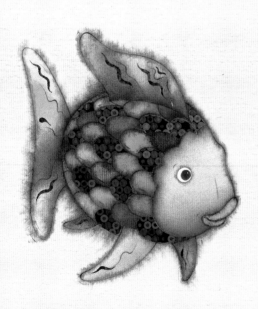

AUTHOR'S NOTE

What was the origin of *The Rainbow Fish?*

Is the account I always give actually true, or is it just a myth that's somehow fixed itself in my mind over the last thirty years? We don't get any younger, but at least our long-term memory ought to keep functioning properly!

Here is how I think it all happened… Brigitte Sidjanski, cofounder and at that time editor of NordSüd Verlag, wanted me to write something along the lines of my first book, *The Sleepy Owl*. And then at some time the cover of that book must have been lying on my desk at an angle of about 90 degrees–the same desk that I've been using for the last thirty years for my stories and illustrations.

And that's how the little owl turned into a fish, which then set out to conquer the world–or at least to win the hearts of lots of children and grown-ups.

Of course the story is about sharing–but not just that. For me it's the first part of the book that's more important. Wealth, beauty, a great pair of sneakers, or the latest mobile phones are no reason to look down on others, to feel and behave as if we're superior. It's what we think and what we do that determines what sort of person we are.

Right from the start, the other fish in the shoal want to play with Rainbow Fish, even without asking him to give away any of his shiny scales. Rainbow Fish could have kept his scales or given them away–whichever he wanted. The decisive factor was his change of heart, with the realization that arrogance, selfishness, and an excessive desire for admiration are of no help if you want to share your life with friends. Perhaps that's also what has made him such a sympathetic character.

Rainbow Fish is not some classical superhero like Robin Hood or Batman. He's a character with weaknesses who sometimes makes mistakes but is able to change and to develop.

This year the walls of a children's hospital in Chile are being painted with pictures of him, a diving club in Thailand has been named after him, in Kathmandu he's being celebrated at a little book festival, and in Germany there's an association for the visually impaired that bears his name.

The little fish has grown up.
I'm proud of him.

Marcus Pfister

LIST OF SOURCES

The selected stories in this volume were written and illustrated by Marcus Pfister.

The Rainbow Fish
Copyright © 1992 by NordSüd Verlag AG, CH-8050 Zürich, Switzerland.

First published in Switzerland under the title *Der Regenbogenfisch*.

English translation copyright © 1992 by NorthSouth Books Inc., New York 10016.
Translated by J. Alison James

Rainbow Fish and the Big Blue Whale
Copyright © 1998 by NordSüd Verlag AG, CH-8050 Zürich, Switzerland.

First published in Switzerland under the title *Der Regenbogenfisch stiftet Frieden*.
English translation copyright © 1998
by NorthSouth Books, Inc., New York 10016. Translated by J. Alison James

Rainbow Fish Discovers the Deep Sea
Copyright © 2009 by NordSüd Verlag AG, CH-8050 Zürich, Switzerland.
First
published in Switzerland under the title *Der Regenbogenfisch entdeckt die Tiefsee*.
English translation copyright © 2009 by NorthSouth Books, Inc., New York 10016.

You Can't Win Them All, Rainbow Fish
Copyright © 2017 by NordSüd Verlag AG, CH-8050 Zürich, Switzerland.

First published in Switzerland under the title *Der Regenbogenfisch lernt verlieren*.
English translation copyright © 2017
by NorthSouth Books Inc., New York 10016. Translated by David Henry Wilson

Good Night, Little Rainbow Fish
Copyright © 2012 by NordSüd Verlag AG, CH-8050 Zürich, Switzerland.
First published in Switzerland under the title *Schlaf gut, kleiner Regenbogenfisch*.
English translation copyright © 2012 by NorthSouth Books Inc., New York 10016.
Translated by David Henry Wilson

MARCUS PFISTER was born in Bern, Switzerland. After studying at the Art School of Bern, he apprenticed as a graphic designer and worked in an advertising agency before becoming self-employed in 1984. His debut picture book, *The Sleepy Owl*, was published by NorthSouth in 1986, but his big breakthrough came six years later with *The Rainbow Fish*. To date, Marcus has illustrated over sixty-five books, which have been translated into more than sixty languages and received countless international awards. He lives with his wife, Debora, and their children in Bern.

First published in the United States, Great Britain, Canada, Australia,
and
New Zealand in 2022 by NorthSouth Books, Inc., an imprint of NordSüd Verlag AG,
CH-8050 Zürich, Switzerland.

Distributed in the United States by NorthSouth Books, Inc., New York 10016.
Library of Congress Cataloging-in-Publication Data is available.

ISBN: 978-0-7358-4506-0 (trade edition)

1 3 5 7 9 · 10 8 6 4 2

Printed in China

www.northsouth.com

Meet Marcus Pfister at www.marcuspfister.ch

FSC
www.fsc.org
MIX
Paper from
responsible sources
FSC® C007972

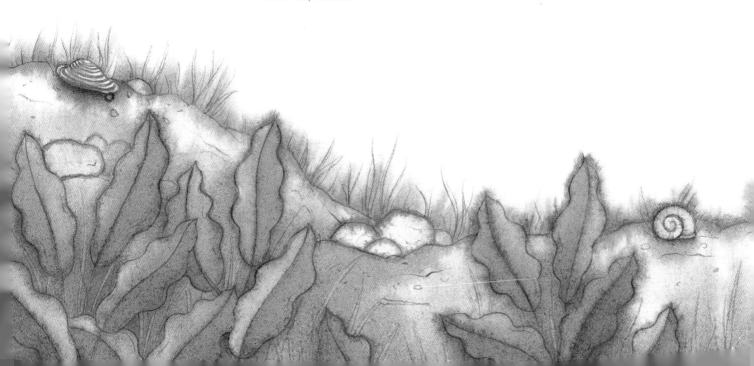